W9-DEW-997

The Cat and the Cuckoo

TED HUGHES

The Cat and the Cuckoo

illustrated by

Flora McDonnell

ROARING BROOK PRESS
BROOKFIELD, CONNECTICUT

Published by Roaring Brook Press
A division of The Millbrook Press
2 Old New Milford Road, Brookfield, Connecticut 06804
First published in 1987 by the Sunstone Press. This edition first published in 2002 by Faber and Faber Limited, London.

Library of Congress Cataloging-in-Publication Data
Hughes, Ted, 1930–
The cat and the cuckoo : collected poems / Ted Hughes
p. cm.
Summary: Illustrated poems about an otter, a dragonfly, a cow, a robin, and many other creatures of land, sea, and air.
1. Animals—Juvenile poetry. 2. Children's poetry, English. [1. Animals—Poetry. 2. English poetry.] I. Title.
PR6058.U37 A6 2002
821'.914—dc21 2001048296

ISBN 0-7613-1548-9 (trade)
2 4 6 8 10 9 7 5 3 1

ISBN 0-7613-2572-7 (library binding)
2 4 6 8 10 9 7 5 3 1

Printed in the United States of America
First American Edition 2003

Contents

for all the children who visit
FARMS FOR CITY CHILDREN

The Cat and the Cuckoo

Cat

You need your Cat.
When you slump down
All tired and flat
With too much town

With too many lifts
Too many floors
Too many neon-lit
Corridors

Too many people
Telling you what
You just must do
And what you must not

With too much headache
Video glow
Too many answers
You never will know

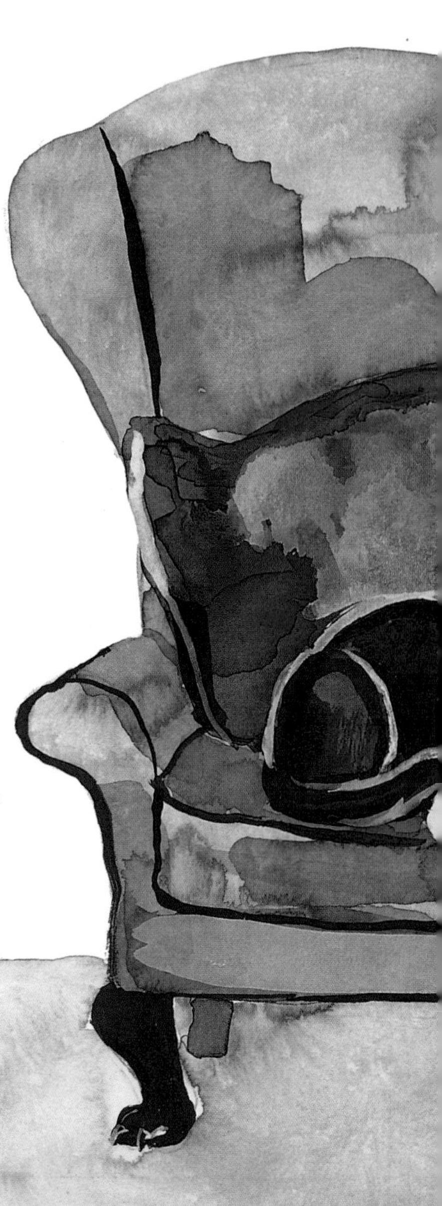

Then stroke the Cat
That warms your knee
You'll find her purr
Is a battery

For into your hands
Will flow the powers
Of the beasts who ignore
These ways of ours

And you'll be refreshed
Through the Cat on your lap
With a Leopard's yawn
And a Tiger's nap.

Toad

The Toad cries: "First I was a thought.
Then that thought it grew a wart.
And the wart had thoughts
Which turned to warts.

I tried to flee
This warty wart
With froggy jumps
But the wart got mumps.
Now this is me.
This lump of bumps
I have to be.

My Consolation Prize
Is ten candlepower eyes.
But where are all the flies?
Eaten by those damned bats!"

His eyes pull down their hats.

Thrush

The speckled Thrush
With a cheerful shout
Dips his beak in the dark
And lifts the sun out.

Then he calls to the Snails:
"God's here again!
Close your eyes for prayers
While I sing Amen.

And after Amen
Rejoice! Rejoice!"

Then he scoops up some dew
And washes his voice.

Goat

Bones. Belly. Bag.
All ridge, all sag.
Lumps of torn hair
Glued here and there.

What else am I
With my wicked eye?

Though nobly born
With a lofty nose
I'm as happy with the Thorn
As I am with the Rose.

Fantails

Up on the roof the Fantail Pigeons dream
Of dollops of curled cream.

At every morning window their soft voices
Comfort all the bedrooms with caresses.

"Peace, peace, peace," through the day
The Fantails hum and murmur and pray.

Like a dream, where resting angels crowded
The roof-slope, that has not quite faded.

When they clatter up, and veer, and soar in a ring
It's as if the house suddenly sang something.

The cats of the house, purring on lap and knee,
Dig their claws and scowl with jealousy.

Pig

I am the Pig.

I saw in my sleep
A dreadful egg.

What a thing to have seen!
And what can it mean

That the Sun's red eye
Which seems to fry
In the dawn sky
So frightens me?

Why should that be?
The meaning is deep.

Upward at these
Hard mysteries

A humble hog
I gape agog.

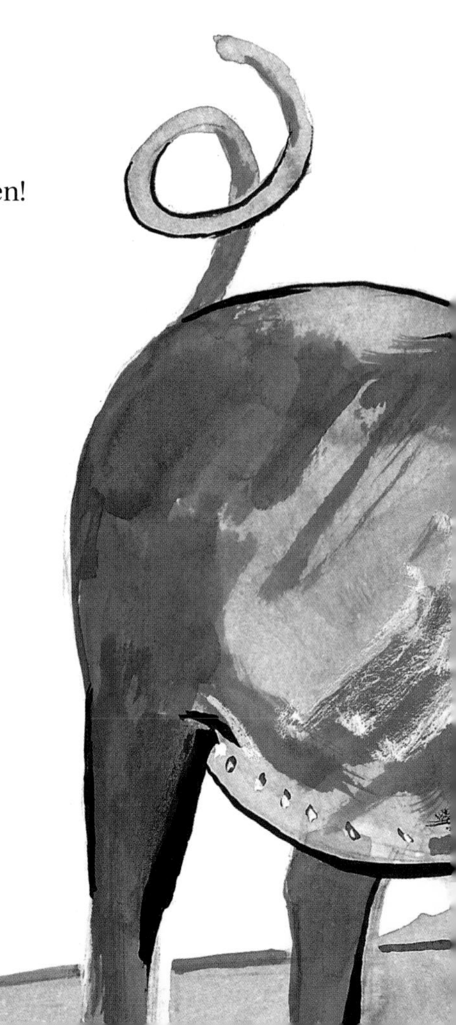

Mole

I am the Mole.
Not easy to know.
Wherever I go
I travel by hole.

My hill-making hand
Is the best of me.
As a seal under sea
I swim under land.

My nose hunts bright
As a beam of light.
With the prick of a pin
My eyes were put in.

Your Telly's there.
You feast as you stare.
Worms are my diet.
In dark and in quiet

I don't eat alone.
At my table sit
Centurion
And Ancient Brit.

Dog

Asleep he wheezes at his ease.
He only wakes to scratch his fleas.

He hogs the fire, he bakes his head
As if it were a loaf of bread.

He's just a sack of snoring dog.
You can lug him like a log.

You can roll him with your foot.
He'll stay snoring where he's put.

Take him out for exercise
He'll roll in cowclap up to his eyes.

He will not race, he will not romp.
He saves his strength for gobble and chomp.

He'll work as hard as you could wish
Emptying the dinner dish.

Then flops flat, and digs down deep,
Like a miner, into sleep.

Cow

The Cow comes home swinging
Her udder and singing:

"The dirt O the dirt
It does me no hurt.

And a good splash of muck
Is a blessing of luck.

O I splosh through the mud
But the breath of my cud

Is sweeter than silk.
O I splush through manure

But my heart stays pure
As a pitcher of milk."

Squirrel

With a rocketing rip
Squirrel will zip
Up a tree-bole
As if down a hole.

He jars to a stop
With tingling ears.
He has two gears:
Freeze and top.

Then up again, plucky
As a jockey
Galloping a Race-
Horse into space.

Dragonfly

Now let's have another try
To love the giant Dragonfly.

Stand beside the peaceful water.
Next thing—a whispy, dry clatter

And he whizzes to a dead stop
In mid-air, and his eyes pop.

Snakey stripes, a snakey fright!
Does he sting? Does he bite?

Suddenly he's gone. Suddenly back. A
Scarey jumping cracker—

Here! Right here!
An inch from your ear!

Sizzling in the air
And giving you a stare

Out of the huge cockpit of his eyes—!

Now say: "What a lovely surprise!"

Robin

When wind brings more snow
To deepen deep snow

Robin busies his beak.
But the pickings are bleak.

He stands at your open door
Asking for more.

"Anything edible?"
He stares towards the table.

The cat can't believe
A bird could be so naïve.

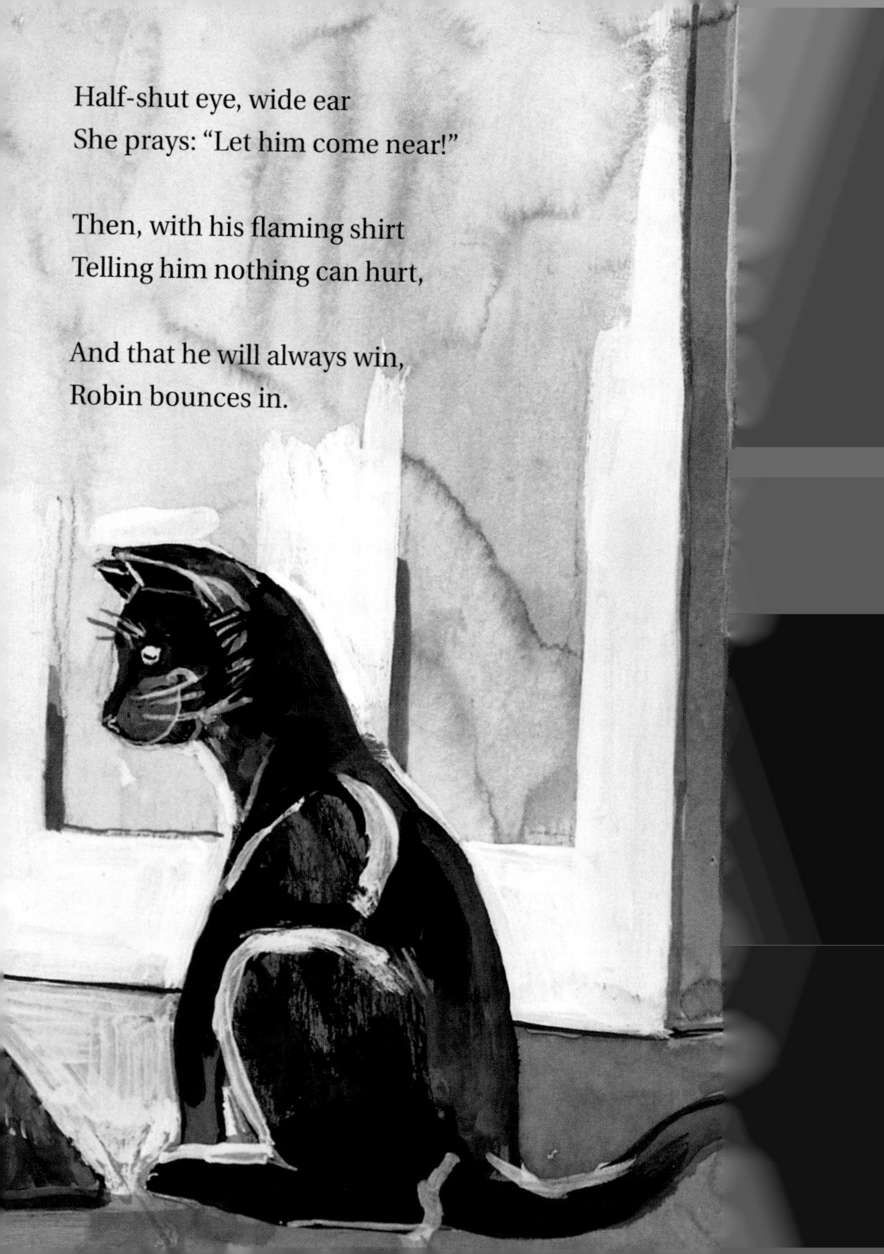

Half-shut eye, wide ear
She prays: "Let him come near!"

Then, with his flaming shirt
Telling him nothing can hurt,

And that he will always win,
Robin bounces in.

Ram

When a Ram can't sleep
He doesn't count Sheep.

He blinks, blinks, blinks,
And he thinks, thinks, thinks

"How has it come to be
That I'm the only Me?

I am, I am, I am
Since I was first a Lamb.

But where was I before?"

Then he snores a gentle snore

And hears, deep in his sleep
A million, million Sheep

Each one bleating: "Why
Am I the only I?"

Otter

An Otter am I,
High and dry
Over the pebbles
See me hobble.
My water-bag wobbles
Until I spill
At the river sill
And flow away thin
As an empty skin
That dribbles bubbles.

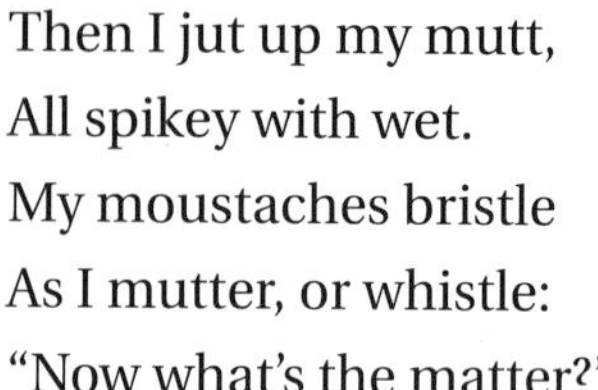

Then I jut up my mutt,
All spikey with wet.
My moustaches bristle
As I mutter, or whistle:
“Now what’s the matter?”

(For that is my song.
Not very long.
There might be a better
Some wetter, wittier
Otter could utter.)

Crow

Thrice, thrice, thrice, the coal-bright Crow
Baaarks–aaarks–aaarks, like a match being struck
To look for trouble.

"Hear ye the Preacher:
Nature to Nature
Returns each creature."

The Crow lifts a claw—
A crucifix
Of burnt matchsticks.

"I am the Priest.
For my daily bread
I nurse the dead."

The monkish Crow
Ruffles his cloak
Like a burnt bible.

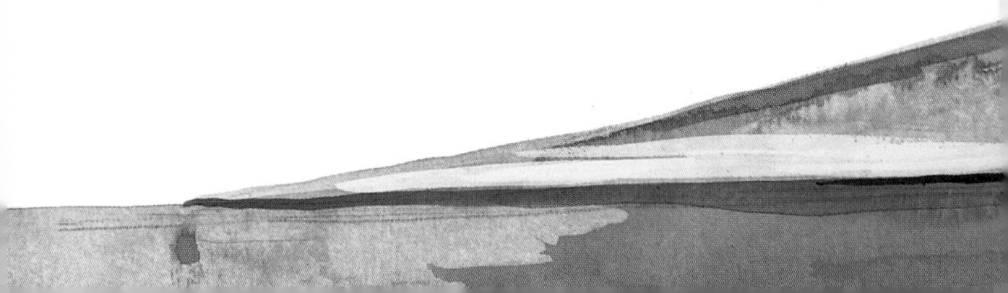

“At my humble feast
I am happy to drink
Whatever you think.”

Then the Crow
Laughs through his hacker
And grows blacker.

Hen

Dowdy the Hen
Has nothing to do
But peer and peck, and peck and peer
At nothing.

Sometimes a couple of scratches to right
Sometimes a couple of scratches to left
And sometimes a head-up, red-rimmed stare
At nothing.

O Hen in your pen, O Hen, O when
Will something happen?
Nothing to do but brood on her nest
And wish.

Wish? Wish? What shall she wish for?
Stealthy fingers
Under her bum.
An egg on your dish.

Pike

I am the Pike.
O you who walk
On two legs and talk
Do not know what I'm like.

You think I'm a cruel
Robot shark
Grabbing fish in the dark
To be my fuel.

No, no! I laze
Through the blazing June days.

On, on, all Summer
I sunbathe in bliss
And gaze at the sky
And pray to become a
Dragonfly.

Remember this
When you say that my fangs
Are solid hunger-pangs,
And that my work
Is murder in the murk,
And that I draw my wages
In the Dark Ages.

Sparrow

Sparrow squats in the dust
Begging for a crust.

"Help an old soldier," he cries.
He doesn't care if he lies.

All he wears on his back
Is a raggy sack.

All day the same old shout:
"I'm back from the wars, worn out!"

Though it looks like shirking
He works at it like working.

Later, on the chimney pot
He takes his sauna very hot.

The Red Admiral

This butterfly
Was the ribbon tie

On the Paradise box
Of Paradise chocs.

O where's the girl
Who wouldn't go bare

As a thistle to wear
Such a bow in her hair.

Shrew

Shrill and astonishing the shrew
Dashes through the early dew.

He's a famine on four feet:
"Something to eat! Something to eat!"

His scream is thinner than a pin
And hurts your ear when it goes in.

And when he meets another shrew
He doesn't rear on hinder toes

And nose to tender, waggling nose
Gently ask: "How do you do?"

He draws a single, furious breath
And fights the other to the death.

Owl

Owl! Owl!
A merry lad!
When he thinks "Good!"
It comes out "Bad!"

The poor Mouse cries:
"Please let me go!"
And Owl thinks "Yes"
But it comes out "No!"

OH NO! OH NO!
OH NO! OH NO!
HO HO! HO HO!
HO HO! HO HO!

"O rest your head,
You silly fellow,
Upon this lovely
Feather Pillow!"

Stickleback

The Stickleback's a spikey chap,
Worse than a bit of briar.
Hungry Pike would sooner swallow
Embers from a fire.

The Stickleback is fearless in
The way he loves his wife.
Every minute of the day
He guards her with his life.

She, like him, is dressed to kill
In stiff and steely prickles,
And when they kiss, there bubbles up
The laughter of the tickles.

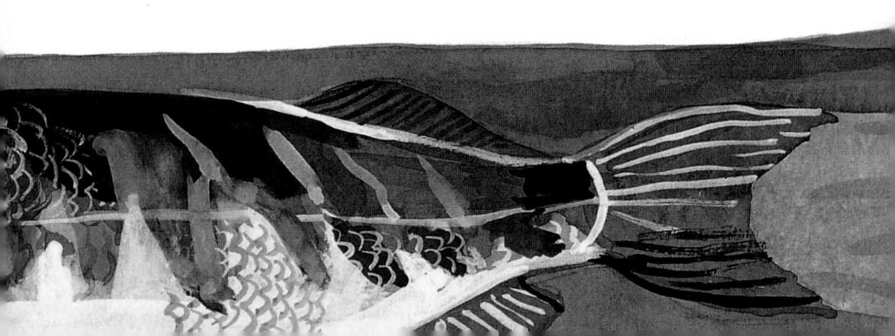

Donkey

The Horse on giant, steely springs
Bounds all over the place.
It circles and circles and circles the globe
In an endless, panting race.

But the Donkey's huge strength
Is already here
At the end of the Horse's journeys,
Asleep, drooping one ear.

Worm

Lowly, slowly,
A pink, wet worm
Sings in the rain:
"O see me squirm

Along the path.
I warp and wind.
I'm searching hard.
If I could find

My elbow, my hair,
My hat, my shoe,
I'd look as pretty
As you, and you."

Hedgehog

The Hedgehog has Itchy the Hedgehog to hug
And a hedgehog bug has a hedgehog bug.

Hedgehog with Hedgehog is happy at ease
And Hedgehogs with fleas, and fleas with fleas.

The batch of the Flea's eggs hatch in the crutch
Of the Hedgehog's armpit, a hot, rich hutch.

The Hedgehog's clutch of hoglets come
In the niche of a ditch, from the Hedgepig's tum.

And so they enjoy their mutual joke
With a pricklety itch and a scratchety poke.

Cuckoo

The Cuckoo's the crookedest, wickedest bird.
His song has two notes, but only one word.

He says to the Linnet: "Your eggs look so ill!
Now I am the Doctor, and here is my pill."

Within that pill, the Cuckoo-child
Crouches hidden, wicked and wild.

He bursts his shell, and with weightlifter's legs
He flings from the nest the Linnet's eggs.

Then bawls to the Linnet: "Look at me, Mam!
How quickly I've grown, and how hungry I am!"

She thinks he is hers, she is silly with joy.
She wears herself bare for the horrible boy.

Till one day he burps, with a pitiless laugh,
"I've had enough of this awful Caf!"

And away he whirls, to Cuckooland,
And leaves her to weep with a worm in her hand.

Peacock

A perfect Peacock on the lawn
  Pranced proudly through his paces.
Pecked at old pancakes, flared his fan
  Like a hand of neon aces.

But while we smiled, he sidled in
  To the nursery flowerbed.
With quivering crown and scabby cheeks
  He pecked off every head.

He slept in the wood. His shawl of eyes
  Drooped to the woodland floor.
O much as we admired his plumes
  A Fox admired him more.

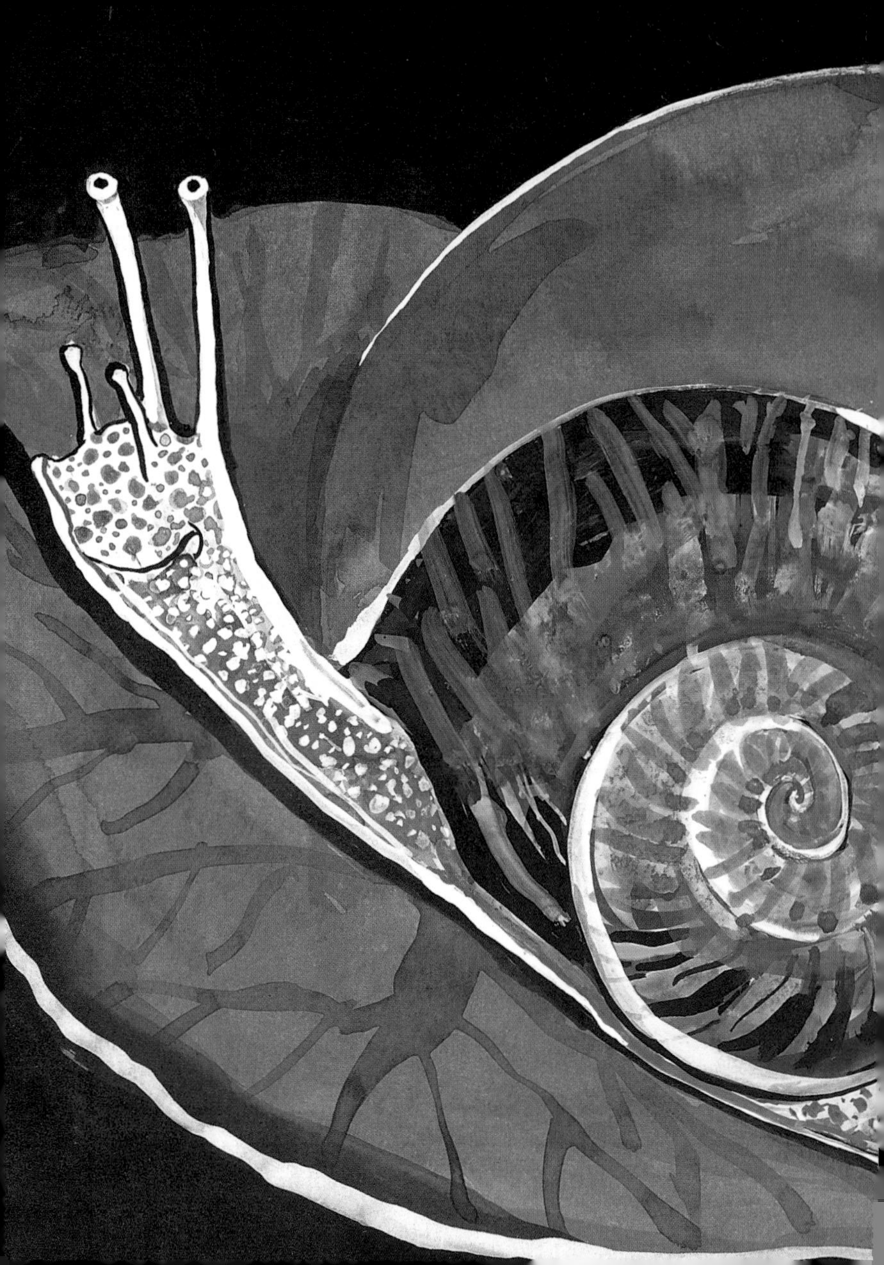

Snail

With skin all wrinkled
Like a Whale
On a ribbon of sea
Comes the moonlit Snail.

The Cabbage murmurs:
"I feel something's wrong!"
The Snail says "Shhh!
I am God's tongue."

The Rose shrieks out:
"What's this? O what's this?"
The Snail says: "Shhh!
I am God's kiss."

So the whole garden
(Till stars fail)
Suffers the passion
Of the Snail.